UNDERPANTS
WONDERPANTS

First published by Parragon in 2013
Parragon
Chartist House
15–17 Trim Street
Bath BA1 1HA, UK
www.parragon.com

Written by Peter Bently   Illustrated by Deborah Melmon
Edited by Laura Baker   Designed by Ailsa Cullen
Production by Richard Wheeler

ISBN 978-1-4723-1997-5

Printed in China

UNDERPANTS
WONDERPANTS

PaRRagon
Bath • New York • Singapore • Hong Kong • Cologne • Delhi
Melbourne • Amsterdam • Johannesburg • Shenzhen

Is it an eagle?

Is it a plane?

NO – it's **underpants wonderpants** to the **rescue** again!

Whenever you
need him,

in **sun,**

snow

or **shower,**

he'll **sort** out your

problems with

UNDERPANTS POWER!

"Elephant **sat** on our nest!"
grumbles Mouse.

"No problem!" says WONDERPANTS.

ZAP!

An **underpants** house!

Polar Bear Cub
can't keep up in the **storm**.

ZAP!
Thanks to **wonderpants** she's **cosy**
and **warm!**

Kangaroo cries,
"I've been **itching**
all night!"

ZAP!

In this hammock,
the insects can't **bite!**

The fisherman's
ripped a **big** hole
in his net. ZAP!

"Thank you, **WONDERPANTS!** It's my **biggest** catch yet!"

"Help!" cries the Queen.
It's so far to the ground —

Wonderpants' Pantachute helps her land safe and **sound!**

Wonderpants zooms to the river,
and in a **great swoop** –

he puts out
the **fire** with his
SUPER-PANT-SCOOP!

But that's not
the **end** of his
super-pants day...

An **alien**
spaceship
is heading
this way!

The **creatures** are

grinning and **shaking**

with **mirth:**
"As soon as we **land**

we'll take over the **EARTH!**"

But **imagine** the look on
each **alien's** face

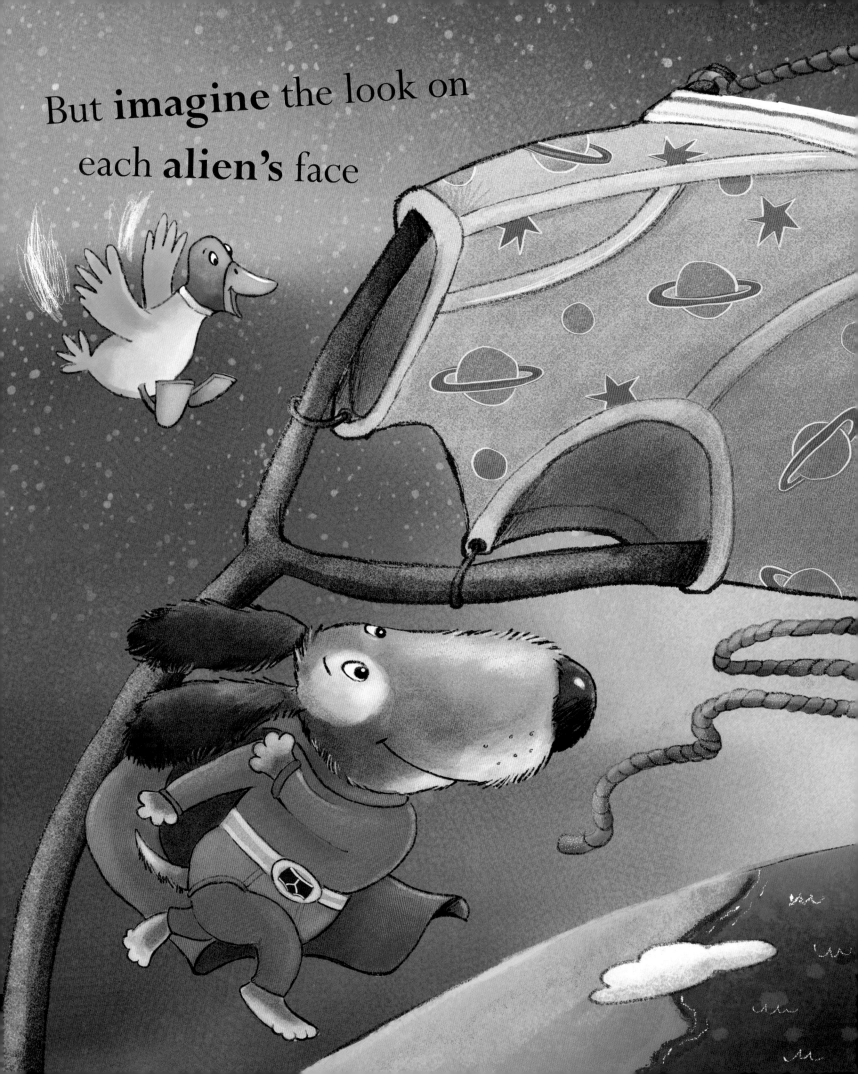

when a **WONDERPANTS**

sling sends them — **ZAP!** — back to **space!**

The people all **cheer**

as they **watch** from afar:

"**WONDERPANTS**
saved us all —

"He's our
SUPER-PANTS STAR!"